19. OCT '16.		
17. FEB 17.		
28/3/19		

Also by Malorie Blackman

The NOUGHTS & CROSSES sequence:
NOUGHTS & CROSSES
KNIFE EDGE
CHECKMATE
DOUBLE CROSS

NOBLE CONFLICT

BOYS DON'T CRY

THE STUFF OF NIGHTMARES
TRUST ME
PIG-HEART BOY
HACKER
A.N.T.I.D.O.T.E.
THIEF!
DANGEROUS REALITY
THE DEADLY DARE MYSTERIES
DEAD GORGEOUS
UNHEARD VOICES
(A collection of short stories and poems, collected by Malorie Blackman)

For younger readers:
CLOUD BUSTING
OPERATION GADGETMAN!
WHIZZIWIG and WHIZZIWIG RETURNS
GIRL WONDER AND THE TERRIFIC TWINS
GIRL WONDER'S WINTER ADVENTURES
GIRL WONDER TO THE RESCUE

BETSEY BIGGALOW IS HERE!
BETSEY BIGGALOW THE DETECTIVE
BETSEY'S BIRTHDAY SURPRISE
MAGIC BETSEY

For beginner readers:
JACK SWEETTOOTH
SNOW DOG
SPACE RACE
THE MONSTER CRISP-GUZZLER

Hurricane Betsey

Malorie
Blackman

Illustrated by Jamie Smith

RED FOX

HURRICANE BETSEY
A RED FOX BOOK 978 1 782 95186 5

First published in Great Britain in 1993 by Piccadilly Press Ltd

This edition published by Red Fox,
an imprint of Random House Children's Publishers UK
A Penguin Random House Company

Penguin
Random House
UK

This Red Fox edition published 2014

1 3 5 7 9 10 8 6 4 2

Text copyright © Oneta Malorie Blackman, 1993
Illustrations copyright © Jamie Smith, 2014

The right of Malorie Blackman to be identified as the author of this work has been
asserted in accordance with the Copyright, Designs and Patents Act 1988.

The Random House Group Limited supports the Forest Stewardship Council® (FSC®),
the leading international forest-certification organisation. Our books carrying the FSC
label are printed on FSC®-certified paper. FSC is the only forest-certification scheme
supported by the leading environmental organisations, including Greenpeace. Our paper
procurement policy can be found at www.randomhouse.co.uk/environment.

MIX
Paper from
responsible sources
FSC® C018179

Set in Bembo MT

RANDOM HOUSE CHILDREN'S PUBLISHERS UK
61–63 Uxbridge Road, London W5 5SA

www.**randomhousechildrens**.co.uk
www.**totallyrandombooks**.co.uk
www.**randomhouse**.co.uk

Addresses for companies within The Random House Group Limited can be found at:
www.randomhouse.co.uk/offices.htm

THE RANDOM HOUSE GROUP Limited Reg. No. 954009

A CIP catalogue record for this book is available from the British Library.

Printed and bound in Great Britain by CPI Group (UK) Ltd, Croydon CR0 4YY

For Neil and Lizzy,
with love as always.

Malorie Blackman has written over sixty books and is acknowledged as one of today's most imaginative and convincing writers for young readers. She has been awarded numerous prizes for her work, including the Red House Children's Book Award and the Fantastic Fiction Award. Malorie has also been shortlisted for the Carnegie Medal. In 2005 she was honoured with the Eleanor Farjeon Award in recognition of her contribution to children's books, and in 2008 she received an OBE for her services to children's literature. She has been described by *The Times* as 'a national treasure'. Malorie Blackman is the Children's Laureate 2013–15.

Contents

Betsey Plays Finders, Keepers!   1

Hurricane Betsey!   16

Betsey and the Insult Contest   29

Betsey and the Monster Hamburger   44

Betsey Plays Finders, Keepers!

"It's mine! It's mine! I found it! Finders, keepers!" said Betsey.

Sherena, Betsey's bigger sister, raised her head from her history homework book.

"What have you found?" asked Sherena.

"This shell necklace. Isn't it pretty?" Betsey replied. She held it up for her sister to see. "I found it here on my bed."

"Betsey, you know very well that necklace is mine." Sherena frowned.

"No I don't." Betsey shook her head. "It hasn't got your name on it and it was on *my* bed. So it's mine! Finders, keepers!"

"Betsey, you toad! Give that back," ordered Sherena.

"Won't! Won't! Won't!" said Betsey.

Sherena stood up, her eyes flashing like lightning. "Betsey, I'm warning you. Give that back."

"Gran'ma . . . GRAN'MA!" Betsey yelled. And she ran out into the living-room with Sherena chasing after her, trying to snatch back her necklace.

"What on earth is going on?" asked Gran'ma Liz.

"Tell Betsey to give me back my necklace, before I get annoyed," said Sherena crossly.

"It's not her necklace. It was on my bed. It's mine! Finders, keepers!" said Betsey.

Gran'ma Liz frowned. "Betsey child! You know as well as I do that that necklace belongs to your sister. Give it back."

"But Gran'ma . . ."

"Elizabeth Ruby Biggalow! Give it back. Don't let me have to tell you again," said Gran'ma Liz.

There was Gran'ma using Betsey's whole, full name! That meant that Betsey had better step carefully or her next step might get her into a lot of TROUBLE!

"Botheration!" Betsey muttered under her breath. Reluctantly, she handed the necklace back to Sherena.

"Hhumph!" said Sherena, before marching back to her bedroom.

Betsey wandered out into the back yard, muttering to herself all the while.

"I *found* that shell necklace on *my* bed," Betsey said to herself. "So it should've been mine. It didn't have Sherena's name on it ..."

Then Betsey spied a cricket ball, lying in the middle of the yard. She ran over to it and picked it up.

"I found it! It's mine! Finders, keepers!" Betsey smiled.

"What are you mumbling about?" Desmond, Betsey's bigger brother, called out from across the back yard.

"Look what I've found, Desmond," beamed Betsey. And she held up the

cricket ball for her brother to see.

Desmond frowned. "You've found my cricket ball there because that's where I put it."

"This cricket ball was lying there, waiting for someone to find it – and that's me!" said Betsey. "This is my cricket ball now."

"Betsey, give me back my ball," said Desmond.

"I won't! It doesn't have your name on it!" Betsey replied.

"Betsey, I'm warning you ..." Desmond said.

"Won't! Won't! Won't!" said Betsey. "This ball is mine."

"Right!" And with that, Desmond started chasing Betsey all around the garden. Betsey ducked around the bread-fruit tree and ran through the chickens

with Desmond racing after her.

"BETSEY! COME BACK HERE!"
Desmond yelled.

Betsey ran into the house, followed by
her brother.

"Wait a minute!" said Gran'ma Liz. "If
you two want to chase each other then
go and do it in the back yard, not in the
house."

"Gran'ma Liz! Tell Betsey to give me

back my ball," Desmond said.

"It's not his ball. I found it in the back yard," Betsey argued.

"Betsey! What has got into you today?" asked Gran'ma Liz. "You know as well as I do that that ball belongs to your brother."

"But . . ."

"No 'buts'!" said Gran'ma Liz. "Give Desmond back his ball."

And although Betsey huffed and puffed and pouted, she had to hand over the cricket ball. Sherena came out of her bedroom just as Betsey went out into the back yard.

"What's going on?" Sherena asked.

"Betsey's playing silly games," sniffed Desmond. "She took my cricket ball and insisted it was hers just because I wasn't holding it at the time."

"She did the same thing to me. She said

my shell necklace was hers just because I didn't put my name on it," said Sherena.

"I think it's time we taught Betsey Biggalow a lesson." Gran'ma Liz winked.

So Sherena and Desmond gathered around her as Gran'ma Liz told them of her plan.

That evening, Uncle George came round for dinner. While Betsey was out of the room, Gran'ma Liz grabbed Uncle George for a quick, secret chat. Then they all sat down to dinner – and what a dinner it was too! Vegetable and dumpling soup, the way only Gran'ma Liz and Mum could make it.

"Betsey, what have you been up to today?" asked Uncle George.

Betsey glanced at Sherena who was staring at her. Then Betsey glanced at Desmond who was glaring at her.

"Er . . . nothing much, Uncle George," said Betsey, taking another spoonful of her soup.

"Betsey! What's that behind you?" Sherena suddenly called out.

Betsey quickly turned her head. "Where? Where?"

"Over there," said Sherena, pointing to the corner of the ceiling.

"I can't see anything." Betsey frowned. Betsey turned back to her soup. The bowl was empty . . . Betsey stared and stared, but it didn't help. Her bowl was still empty.

"Where's my soup gone?" Betsey asked, amazed.

"Oh, was it your soup?" asked Uncle George. "I didn't know that. It was just sitting on the table, so I helped myself."

"But . . . but . . . that was *my* soup," Betsey spluttered.

"It didn't have your name on it, Betsey," said Gran'ma Liz. "So how was your uncle to know it was yours?"

"Because . . . because . . . the bowl was in front of me," said Betsey.

"But the whole table is in front of me. So the table and everything on it is mine," said Uncle George. "Finders, keepers!"

"But that's not fair," said Betsey.

"In fact, not only does the table and everything on it belong to me, but everyone at the table belongs to me too!" said Uncle George.

And Uncle George stood up and went over to Betsey. Before she could say "dumplings!", Uncle George picked her up and threw her over his shoulder.

"Look what I've found, everyone!" Uncle George grinned. "This girl was just sitting here and I found her. As she hasn't got anyone's name on her, I'm going to keep her. Finders, keepers!"

"You can keep her for as long as you like, Uncle!" said Desmond.

"Uncle! Uncle! Put me down," yelled Betsey.

"Who said that?" said Uncle George, looking around.

"I said it, Uncle George. Put me down," said Betsey.

"Why?"

"Because I . . . I don't belong to you," said Betsey.

"Who do you belong to then?" asked Uncle George.

"I belong to . . . myself," Betsey decided.

"Where does it say that?" asked Uncle George.

"It doesn't say that anywhere. But it's true," said Betsey.

"What about this shell necklace? Whose is it?" asked Sherena, holding up the necklace for Betsey to see.

"It's yours. Mum gave it to you for your last birthday," Betsey replied.

Desmond held up a cricket ball. "And who does this belong to?" he asked.

"It's yours," said Betsey. "It's the special one Dad bought for you."

"So have we heard the last of this finders, keepers nonsense?" asked Gran'ma Liz.

"Yes! Yes! I'm never going to say those two words ever, *ever* again," said Betsey.

"In that case, I'll put you down," said Uncle George. And he put Betsey back on her feet.

"And I'll give you some more soup!"

Gran'ma Liz smiled.

Gran'ma Liz filled Betsey's bowl with some soup from the pot. Betsey helped herself to some more dumplings.

When Sherena finished her soup, she peered into the pot.

"Gran'ma Liz, are there any more dumplings left?" asked Sherena.

"Sorry, Sherena. Betsey had the last one," Gran'ma Liz replied.

"Finders, keepers!" said Betsey.

Hurricane Betsey!

"Sherena, Desmond, Betsey, come in here a minute," called Mum.

Sherena came in from the back yard where she was polishing her bike. Desmond came in from his bedroom where he was doing his homework — for once! Betsey was already in the living-room.

"What's the matter, Mum?" asked Sherena.

Mum looked very worried.

"I've got some bad news," said Mum at last. "There's just been a hurricane warning on the TV. Hurricane Boris is heading this way."

"A hurricane?" asked Betsey.

"Oh, you've never seen a hurricane, have you?" said Desmond, his eyes big and round like saucers. "A hurricane is like a huge, ferocious storm with winds gusting at over one hundred and fifteen kilometres an hour. The winds are so strong, they can lift you right off your feet and they can blow down trees and blow the roofs off houses and make the sea spin like it's being stirred by a giant spoon . . ."

"That's quite enough, Desmond," said Mum sternly.

"Will we spin up and up in the air as well?" asked Betsey quickly.

"Of course not," said Mum. "As long as we stay in the house, we'll be fine."

"But I *want* to spin up and up in the air," said Betsey, very disappointed. "I want to fly."

"Then you'll just have to wait until you fly in an aeroplane like the rest of us," said Sherena. "If a hurricane spun you up in the air, when you landed you'd probably break almost every bone in your body . . ."

"That's quite enough from you as well, Sherena." Mum frowned.

"What should we do, Mum?" asked Desmond.

"I want the three of you to help me pack away all the breakable things," said Mum.

Betsey stared and stared.

"What's the matter, Betsey?" asked Mum.

"I don't want to be packed away! I don't want to be packed away!"

Betsey sniffed, very close to tears.

Everyone burst out laughing.

"Betsey, child! We're not going to pack *you* away," said Gran'ma Liz.

"We'd never find a box big enough!" muttered Desmond.

"We're going to pack up my best plates and glasses and anything else that's fragile," Mum told Betsey.

"Fragile?" said Betsey.

"That means easily breakable," Sherena told her. "And Betsey, you *aren't* fragile!"

So that's what they did. Betsey and Sherena and Desmond wrapped up Mum's best glasses and plates and ornaments in newspaper before packing them into boxes.

"Mum, where do we go so we don't get swirled and whirled up into the air?"

"We'll stay in the living-room," Mum answered.

"Will we be safe?" asked Betsey, anxiously.

"Of course. We'll be together, won't we?" Gran'ma Liz smiled.

"Sherena, bring your bike in from outside, and Betsey, go and get Prince from the back yard, please," said Mum.

Prince was the family Alsatian dog.

Betsey ran out into the back yard to fetch him. Once outside, Betsey noticed that the leaves of the breadfruit tree were jiggling madly, as if dancing to some music that Betsey couldn't hear.

"A hurricane is coming! A hurricane is coming!" Betsey shouted out.

And she whirled and twirled around, knocking the flowerpots off the ledge beside her.

"BETSEY! Bring Prince inside and stop dancing about," said Gran'ma Liz. "Hurricanes are serious business and nothing to be glad about."

"Yes, Gran'ma," said Betsey.

Betsey looked up at the sky. It was dark and grey and she couldn't see the sun. A drop of water landed on her forehead, then another drop landed on her cheek. The storm was beginning. Betsey called Prince over and together they went into the house.

"What else should I do, Mum?" asked Betsey.

"Now we have to board up all the windows so that they don't blow in on us," said Mum, looking around. "Sherena, Gran'ma and I will do that. You and Desmond fill all the flasks in the house with water. Then make sure that the bath tub and the sink are clean and fill them with cold water as well."

"Why do we have to do that?" asked Betsey.

"The hurricane might disrupt the water supply, so we should make sure we've got enough drinking water to last us for a while," Mum explained.

For the rest of the morning, the whole family was busy, busy, busy, but at last everything was done.

"Desmond, bring your homework in

here so you can carry on with it," said Gran'ma Liz.

"Do I have to?" Desmond pleaded.

"Yes you do. Sherena, if you've got any homework, you might as well do it now too," said Gran'ma Liz.

"We'll all stay in this one room and watch the TV for news of the hurricane," said Mum.

Betsey sat next to Mum, who put her arm around Betsey's shoulders.

"Will we be all right?" Betsey whispered.

"Of course we will." Mum smiled.

Outside, Betsey could hear the heavy rain splashing against the roof and the windows and she could hear the wind howling around the house.

"Please stay in your homes and listen to your radios or your TVs for further information. Please do not use your phones unless it is an emergency. Please stay in your homes and

listen to your radios or your TVs for further information."

"What's that?" Betsey squeaked.

"Don't worry, Betsey. It's just the police, advising people about what they should do," said Mum. "They'll drive around for as long as they can, talking through a loudspeaker so that everyone can hear them."

"Oh!" said Betsey, and she cuddled up closer to Mum.

A while later, an announcement came on TV.

"This is a hurricane update. The hurricane has changed course and is now heading out to sea. Repeat. The hurricane has changed course and is now heading out to sea."

"Thank goodness for that." Gran'ma Liz gave a sigh of relief.

"We're still going to get stormy weather for a while but at least the hurricane won't be passing this way," said Mum. "OK, everyone, let's start unpacking the boxes and putting everything back in its place."

Betsey sprang up off the sofa and ran to the nearest box.

"I'll help. Let me help," she said, picking up the box which was filled with a few cups and saucers wrapped in newspaper. Betsey whirled and twirled around with the box in her hands. "The hurricane has gone! The hurricane has gone!" she grinned. But because of the box, Betsey didn't see that she was heading straight for Prince . . .

"No, Betsey . . ."

"Don't . . ."

Too late. Betsey tripped over Prince and the box of cups and saucers in her hands went flying up into the air to land with an enormous **SMAAAAASH-CRAAAAASH!** All of the crockery in the box was shattered!

Betsey stared at the mess at her feet.

"Is everyone all right? No one got cut, did they?" asked Mum.

Everyone was fine – except Betsey.

"Mum, it wasn't me. It was . . ." Betsey began.

"Betsey, sit on the sofa and watch the TV," interrupted Gran'ma Liz. "You're causing more damage than the hurricane would've done! In fact I know what we should call you . . ."

And everyone shouted out, "Hurricane Betsey!"

Betsey and the Insult Contest

Betsey came home from school, with her chin drooping and her mouth frowning and tears in her eyes.

"Betsey child, what's the matter with you?" asked Gran'ma Liz, immediately concerned.

"I . . . I had a quarrel with May," Betsey whispered.

"A quarrel? What about?" asked Gran'ma.

Betsey didn't answer. She just shook her head and stared down at her sandals.

That evening, Betsey hardly touched

her dinner. It was one of her favourites too — flying fish and French fries and fresh salad. There was a huge jug of orange juice in the middle of the table but Betsey didn't ask for seconds and thirds the way she usually did. She drank half a glass of orange juice and left the rest. Gran'ma Liz and Sherena and Desmond looked at each other, then at Betsey. They were beginning to get worried.

After dinner Betsey moped around the house, sighing and sniffing and not saying a word, until Desmond and Sherena couldn't stand it any more.

"Betsey, what did you and May have an argument about?" asked Sherena.

"Nothing much," Betsey replied.

"Go on. You can tell us. Why did you and May have a bust up?" Desmond asked.

"I'm not telling you," sniffed Betsey.

"Come on, Betsey. We want to help," said Sherena.

"Yeah! I miss having you bouncing around the house and chatting so much I can't hear myself think," said Desmond.

"So why did you and May fall out?" said Gran'ma Liz.

"It doesn't matter," sighed Betsey. And off she walked.

At last Mum came home, but Betsey wouldn't even tell *her* what was wrong.

She just wandered around the house, her face as long as a tree trunk, saying, "It doesn't matter. It doesn't matter."

"Mum, do something," Sherena whispered, when Betsey couldn't hear.

"She'd driving us nuts!" said Desmond. "I thought Betsey was bad enough when she made a lot of noise, but she's even worse when she's quiet!"

"All right, then," said Mum. "Let me phone up May's mum. Maybe May told her what's going on."

So Mum phoned May's house and was on the phone for quite a while. When at last she put the phone down, Mum had a deep frown on her face.

"Well? What's going on?" asked Gran'ma Liz.

"May won't tell her mum what they quarrelled about either," said Mum. "I think it's time for me to take the matter

into my own hands."

"What d'you mean, Mum?" asked Desmond.

"You'll see." That's all Mum would say.

The next day was a Saturday. A beautiful, sunny Saturday with not a cloud in the sky. Not that Betsey noticed. She moped around the house, quieter than a mouse.

"Betsey, do you want to ride my bike?" Sherena asked.

"No, thank you," said Betsey, her head bent.

Sherena stared at her in amazement. Betsey had never before said no to riding Sherena's bike. Usually Betsey pouted and pestered and badgered and bothered Sherena for a ride, until Sherena usually gave in, just to get some peace.

Betsey wandered out into the back yard.

"Betsey, let's make a bow and some arrows. We could have an archery contest," said Desmond.

"No, thank you," Betsey sighed.

Desmond stared at her in disbelief. Betsey had been asking him to show her how to make a bow and arrow from tree branches for the last month. And now, he'd offered to show her and she'd turned him down flat. Desmond watched as Betsey wandered back into the house.

Later that afternoon, Sherena whispered to Desmond, "Is Betsey back to normal yet?"

"No. And I offered to make a bow and arrow with her," said Desmond.

"I offered her a ride on my bike and she said no," said Sherena.

"This is serious," said Desmond.

And off they went to find Mum.

"Mum, we're worried about Betsey," said Sherena.

Just at that moment, the front door opened.

"We're here!" called out May's mum.

Mum, Sherena and Desmond went out into the living-room. May and her mum were standing there. May and Betsey stood facing each other but neither of them said a word.

"Betsey, say hello to May then," said Mum.

Betsey didn't say a word.

"May, say hello to your friend Betsey," said May's mum.

May turned her head away.

"It was the same thing last night," said May's mum. "May moped around the house and she hardly touched her dinner, but she wouldn't tell me what she and

Betsey had argued about."

"All right then," Betsey's mum said firmly. "Betsey, sit here. May, you sit down next to her."

Betsey sat down on the sofa and May sat down next to her, although they were careful not to touch each other.

"Right then, you two," said Mum. "You're going to have an insult contest."

"An insult contest?" said Betsey, surprised.

"What's that?" asked May.

"Both of you will take it in turns to insult each other. The rest of us are going to sit opposite you and watch and listen. At the end of it we'll judge which one of you has come up with the best insult."

"But . . ."

"Oh, but . . ."

"No buts," said Mum, interrupting both May and Betsey. "Who wants to go first?"

May and Betsey frowned at each other.

"OK, then," said Mum. "As you're the guest, May, you can go first. Think of an insult for Betsey."

May looked at Betsey, before looking down at her hands in her lap. She muttered something under her breath.

"We didn't quite catch that, May" said

Mum. "Please say it again."

"I said that Betsey is a cabbage head," said May, very loudly this time.

"A cabbage head? Well, your head is shaped just like a dog biscuit and your ears are tiny like raisins!" said Betsey, annoyed.

"So my head's like a dog biscuit, is it? Well, you're a . . . a . . . slimy snake . . ." began May.

"Ah! Can't allow that one," Mum interrupted. "Snakes aren't slimy. Their skin is quite dry."

Mum turned to May's mum and Sherena and Desmond. "Do you all agree?" she asked.

They all nodded.

"May, you'll have to come up with another insult," said Mum.

"Betsey is a toad face . . ." said May.

"You're a smelly sock . . ." said Betsey.

"You're a stinky sock . . ."

"You're more stinky than me . . ."

"No I'm not . . ."

"Yes, you are . . ."

"You're a tissue that someone's blown their nose into lots and lots of times . . ." said May.

Something very strange was happening.

May's lips quivered and Betsey's lips twitched with each new insult that they flung at each other.

"You're the inside of Desmond's sweaty, smelly sports bag when he's been

playing cricket," said Betsey.

"Well, you're a . . . a . . ." May began.

"And you're a . . . you're a . . ." Betsey started.

But neither of them finished their insults. They both began to giggle, then to chuckle, then to roar with laughter. Which was just as well, because Betsey's mum and May's mum and Sherena and Desmond were all laughing so hard that they wouldn't have heard the next lot of insults anyway.

"I'm sorry, Betsey." May smiled.

"I'm sorry too." Betsey smiled back.

"So are you two friends again?" asked Mum.

Betsey and May nodded their heads.

"Glad to hear it," said May's mum. "What did you argue about in the first place?"

Betsey and May looked at each other, surprised.

"I can't remember," said Betsey.

"Neither can I!" said May.

"Never mind," said Betsey. "Let's go and play on the beach."

"You bet!" said May.

Betsey and May bounced off the sofa and ran for the front door.

"Before you disappear, Betsey," said Desmond, calling after his sister, "I just want to say one thing."

"What's that?" asked Betsey.

"The inside of my sports bag is not sweaty and smelly!" said Desmond.

"Desmond, go and stick your nose in it and then say that," said Mum. "Betsey described your sports bag perfectly!"

Betsey and the Monster Hamburger

"When we get there, I'm going to have a chicken burger," said Desmond.

"I'm going to have a veggie burger," said Sherena.

"I'm going to have a hamburger," said Betsey. "A big hamburger. The BIGGEST hamburger they've got. A MONSTER hamburger!"

The whole family was going to the local burger bar. For once, neither Mum nor Gran'ma Liz had felt like cooking, so they were all going to eat out. It was a lovely evening. The air was warm and a gentle breeze was blowing.

"I'm going to have a strawberry milk-shake," said Sherena.

"I think I'll have a vanilla one," said Desmond.

"I'm going to have two chocolate milkshakes," said Betsey, skipping down the road.

"Betsey, don't be such a pig," said Desmond.

"You'll never finish two milkshakes. It takes me ages just to finish one and my stomach is a lot bigger than yours," said Sherena.

"I'm going to have two – and you can't stop me," said Betsey.

"Betsey Biggalow, you will have one milkshake and like it," Mum called out.

"But Mum, I'm really hungry," said Betsey.

"One, Betsey," said Mum firmly. "You'll have one milkshake or none at all."

"Botheration!" Betsey muttered under her breath. "I bet if it was Sherena or Desmond, they could have two if they wanted."

"Pardon, Betsey?" said Gran'ma Liz.

"Nothing, Gran'ma," Betsey replied.

Once they reached the burger bar, Mum asked each of them what they wanted. When it was Betsey's turn, Betsey said, "I want a MONSTER hamburger and two chocolate milkshakes and a large

portion of French fries."

"Betsey, you'll have a small portion of French fries and *one* chocolate milk-shake," said Mum.

"But I'm starving."

"Betsey, your trouble is your eyes are bigger than your stomach. I'm not going to buy all that food for you to leave most of it," said Mum.

"Can't I at least have the MONSTER hamburger?" sniffed Betsey.

"You'll never finish it," said Mum.

"I will. I promise," said Betsey. "*Please.*"

"No, Betsey, you can't . . ." Mum began.

"Please, Mum. I will eat it. I'm starving hungry," said Betsey.

Mum frowned down at Betsey.

"All right then, Betsey," Mum said at last. "I'll buy you a MONSTER hamburger and you'd better eat it. I don't want to see any left."

"You won't." Betsey beamed.

"Hhmm!" was all Gran'ma Liz said.

Desmond and Mum went up to the counter to order whilst Gran'ma Liz, Sherena and Betsey found a table. It didn't take long for Mum and Desmond to join them, each carrying a tray filled with food.

Betsey licked her lips. Her very first MONSTER hamburger! She was going to enjoy this!

Mum put Betsey's MONSTER hamburger in front of her.

"There you are, Betsey," said Mum.

"Thanks, Mum." Betsey grinned.

"Eating that will soon wipe the grin off
your face, Elizabeth Ruby Biggalow,"
said Gran'ma Liz.

"Botheration!" said Betsey. "Gran'ma, I
will finish this hamburger. Just watch."

"I intend to," said Gran'ma Liz.

And with that they all started to eat.

Betsey picked up her hamburger with
both hands. She
looked at it from
above, she looked
at it from below, she
checked each side of
it. It was HUGE! In
fact it was so big, she
hardly knew where
to begin.

"Anything wrong, Betsey?" asked Mum.
"No, Mum," Betsey replied.

Then she opened her eyes W-I-D-E
and opened her mouth W-I-D-E-R and
bit into her hamburger. Tomato ketchup
squirted out one side of the hamburger
and hit Desmond – PLOOPPP! – on
the nose. A dollop of mustard flew out of
the other side of the hamburger and hit
Sherena – SPLATTT! – on the forehead.

"Betsey, look what you've done. I look like I've got a nose bleed," said Desmond, annoyed.

"Betsey, watch what you're doing," said Sherena, wiping the mustard off her face.

"Well done, Betsey," laughed Mum. "You managed to get two people with just one bite."

Betsey chewed and chewed away at the piece of hamburger she had managed to bite off. Then she had some French fries and washed it all down with some chocolate milkshake. It was all double delicious! Betsey took another bite and another, then another.

The only trouble was, she was beginning to feel full and she hadn't even eaten half of the burger yet. Betsey chewed more and more slowly, as she became more and more full.

"What's the matter, Betsey? Is that hamburger too much for you?" asked Gran'ma Liz.

"Oh, no, Gran'ma," Betsey replied quickly. "I'm just eating it slowly so that I can remember what every mouthful tastes like."

Gran'ma Liz and Mum exchanged a look.

"Hhmm!" was all Gran'ma said.

What am I going to do? thought Betsey as she chewed on yet another mouthful. She was stuffed! If she had just one more bite, she would pop like a balloon. But if she stopped now, everyone would say, 'We told you so!'

Then Betsey had an idea. She arranged the paper napkin on her lap to cover her skirt. She broke off a bit of her burger. Then she pretended to put the piece of burger into her mouth but she didn't really . . .

Whilst she was pretending to chew, Betsey waited until no one was looking and dropped the little bit of burger from her hand into her napkin. As soon as the coast was clear, Betsey did the same thing again. She broke off a piece and pretended to eat

it, but instead dropped it into her napkin. Ten pieces later, there was no more hamburger left in her hands – but lots of pieces of hamburger sat on the napkin in her lap. Betsey folded up the napkin until none of the hamburger could be seen.

Betsey picked up her chocolate milk-shake and took a long drink. Pretending to eat hamburger was very thirsty work!

"Well done, Betsey!" Mum said, surprised. "I must admit, I didn't think you could do it."

"I told you I was hungry," said Betsey.

"Your appetite has doubled overnight – and so has your stomach," said Gran'ma Liz.

"OK everyone, pass over your napkins and empty wrappers and cups and I'll put them all on this tray," said Mum.

Oh no! thought Betsey. She couldn't hand over her napkin to Mum. Her mum would feel the napkin and immediately guess what was in it. That's when Betsey had another idea.

She deliberately dropped her knife on the floor.

"I'll just pick that up," said Betsey, and

she scooted under the table. Quick as a jack-rabbit, Betsey opened up Sherena's handbag and put in the napkin filled with all the pieces of hamburger. Then she got the knife and sat

up again, putting the knife on one of the trays.

"Come on then, everyone. Let's go home," said Mum. And they all stood up.

On the way home Sherena said, "Well done, Betsey. I didn't think you'd finish that hamburger. I've never been able to finish one of those in my life."

Betsey said nothing. What could she say? And there was just one thing on her mind. How was she going to get the napkin filled with hamburger out of

Sherena's bag without anyone finding out?

Botheration! thought Betsey. Double and triple botheration!

"Sherena, do you want me to carry your handbag?" Betsey asked hopefully.

"What on earth for?" asked Sherena.

"No reason."

"No, thank you," said Sherena.

Just at that moment, Betsey felt the back of her neck go all tingly and hot. She turned around and there was Gran'ma Liz standing right behind her. And Gran'ma Liz had that look in her eyes. The look that said, "Betsey, you're up to something. I don't know what it is, but we both know I'm going to find out!"

And it didn't take her long to find out either! Betsey followed Sherena into the house, hoping for a chance to take her napkin out of Sherena's handbag. But no sooner had they taken just a couple of steps into the house than Prince, the Alsatian dog, came bounding up to Sherena and started sniffing at her handbag.

"Prince, what are you doing?" Sherena frowned.

Prince snatched the handbag and raced off around the living-room with it. Sherena chased after him, followed by Betsey and Desmond.

"What's the matter with that dog?"

"I think I know," said Gran'ma Liz.

"Prince, sit! Sit!"

Immediately Prince did as he was told.

"Sherena, bring me your handbag," said Gran'ma Liz.

Sherena handed over her bag to Gran'ma.

"Now then, Betsey," said Gran'ma Liz. "Is there anything you want to say before I open this handbag?"

"Just that I'm sorry and I won't do it

again," Betsey sniffed.

"Hhmm!" said Gran'ma Liz. And she opened the handbag.

"What's going on?" asked Sherena, puzzled.

Gran'ma Liz looked at Betsey. Betsey looked up at Gran'ma Liz. Gran'ma Liz took the napkin out of Sherena's handbag and put it in her cardigan pocket.

"Nothing's going on," said Gran'ma Liz at last. "Isn't that right, Betsey?"

"That's right, Gran'ma," said Betsey, in a tiny voice.

Betsey couldn't believe it. Gran'ma Liz wasn't going to tell anyone what she'd done!

"Betsey, the next time we go to the burger bar, what are you going to have?" asked Gran'ma Liz.

"One milkshake and a small portion of fries," Betsey replied.

"No MONSTER hamburger?" asked Sherena.

"I don't care if I never see another hamburger again as long as I live," said Betsey.

And she meant it!

Have you read these
Betsey Biggalow books?

Have you read these
Girl Wonder books?

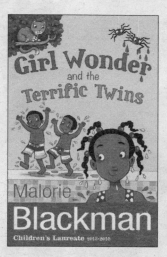

Hurricane Betsey's Windy Wordsearch

There are ten words hidden in this weather-themed wordsearch.
Can you find them all?

1. BORIS
2. CLOUDS
3. GUSTING
4. HURRICANE
5. RAIN
6. SEA
7. SKY
8. STORM
9. WEATHER
10. WIND

W B L J Z N T G H U V C X S W
R I M S R B L U N J E G V D K
A U N M N P R N M I M W O U W
I C I D M R L K M R T E I O I
N J B I I L X X O R E S T L H
Y K S C W A I T Q W C Z U C L
N B A N T C S D B T F N B G W
A N U J W P W A H L D V G Q Q
E L I S R R U F U W A H P V G
M I S O C I J W K V W S I C D
Q I V S E K P L D B K J Z H R
C L E B N M B W C Y N P Y L C
O A F G X S E O V U O X Q U K
V N P J L Q R T L J O H O E Y
R E H T A E W B O R I S W W I

Turn to the back of the book to see the answers!

Hurricane Facts

- A hurricane is a huge storm which forms into a spiral of strong winds and heavy rain.

- Hurricanes always form over the warm oceans around the middle of the Earth because they take their energy from warm air that's full of moisture – think of steam rising from a warm bath. The warm wet air rises and forms into thick storm clouds which spin in the winds that move around the *equator* – the imaginary line which divides the Earth into two halves around its middle.

- As the storm spins, an area of calm forms in the middle – this is called the *eye*. In the northern half of the Earth, called the *Northern Hemisphere*, hurricanes spin anti-clockwise around the eye, while in the *Southern Hemisphere* they spin clockwise.

- Hurricanes can range in size from 100 to 2,000 kilometres across.

- The strength of a hurricane is categorized from 1 to 5, according to the speed of the winds inside the storm. Category 1 hurricanes have wind speeds of around 120 to 150 kilometres per hour, while Category 5 hurricanes have wind speeds of over 250 kilometres per hour.

- Because they need air that is full of water for their energy, hurricanes lose power as they move from over the ocean to over land. But the winds and heavy rains that they bring can do lots of damage to areas where people live.

- Scientists are getting much better at predicting the strength and the direction of hurricanes so that people who live in their paths have time to prepare and protect themselves. But as the world's climate changes there is still a lot of work to be done to keep people safe in the future.

Spot the Difference

There are five differences
between the two pictures below.
Can you spot them all?

Turn to the back of the book to see the answers!

Word Scramble

The names of some of Betsey's family
members have got all jumbled up!
Can you unscramble them all?

CENRIP

_ _ _ _ _

CLUEN EROEGG

_ _ _ _ _   _ _ _ _ _ _

ARNEESH

_ _ _ _ _ _

SNEDOMD

_ _ _ _ _ _

ANGARM ZIL

_ _ _ _ _ _   _ _ _

Turn to the back of the book to see the answers!

Answers

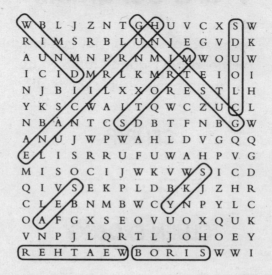

PRINCE

UNCLE GEORGE

SHERENA

DESMOND

GRAN'MA LIZ